A CHILD IS BORN

The Christmas Story

Adapted from
The New Testament
by
Elizabeth Winthrop

illustrated by
Charles Mikolaycak

HOLIDAY HOUSE / NEW YORK

Library of Congress Cataloging in Publication Data

Winthrop, Elizabeth.
A child is born.

Summary: An illustrated retelling of the birth of Jesus.
1. Jesus Christ—Nativity—Juvenile literature.
[1. Jesus Christ—Nativity] I. Mikolaycak, Charles, ill.
II. Title.
BT315.2.W53   1983   226'.09505   82-11728
ISBN 0-8234-0472-2

Elizabeth Winthrop faithfully adapted the Christmas story from The Book of St. Luke, 2:1–2:21, and The Book of St. Matthew, 2:1–2:12, in the King James version of the Bible.

AND it came to pass
in those days,
that there went out a decree
from Caesar Augustus,
that all the world should
be taxed.

And all went to be taxed,
everyone into his own city.
And Joseph went up
from Galilee unto Bethlehem,
to be taxed
with Mary his wife,
being great with child.

*While they were there,
she brought forth her
firstborn son, and wrapped him
in swaddling clothes,
and laid him in a manger
because there was
no room for them in the inn.*

In the same country,
there were shepherds
in the field keeping watch
over their flock by night.

The angel of the Lord
came upon them,
and the glory of the Lord
shone round about them:
and they were afraid.
And the angel said unto them,
"Fear not: for, I bring you
good tidings of great joy.
Unto you is born this day
a Saviour,
which is Christ the Lord.

*Ye shall find the babe
wrapped in swaddling clothes,
lying in a manger."
And suddenly
there was with the angel a
multitude of the heavenly host
praising God, and saying,
"Glory to God in the highest,
and on earth,
peace, good will toward men."*

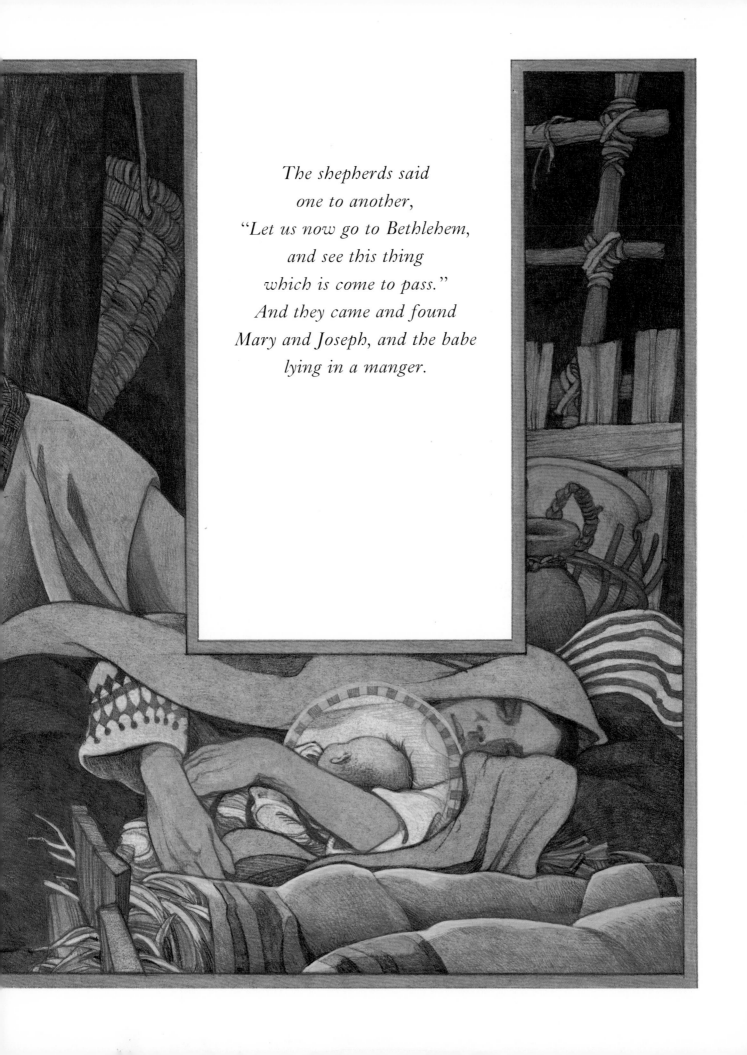

The shepherds said
one to another,
"Let us now go to Bethlehem,
and see this thing
which is come to pass."
And they came and found
Mary and Joseph, and the babe
lying in a manger.

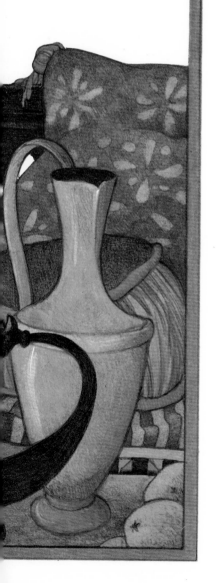

Now when the child was born
in Bethlehem, there
came wise men from the east
saying, "Where is he
that is born King of the Jews?
For we have seen
his star in the east,
and are come to worship him."
When Herod the King
had heard these things,
he was troubled.

*And when he had gathered
all the chief priests
of the people together,
he demanded of them where
Christ should be born.
And they said to him,
"In Bethlehem."
Then Herod called the wise men
and sent them to Bethlehem,
and said, "Go and search
for the young child;
and when ye have found him,
bring me word again
that I may come
and worship him also."*

When they had heard the king,
they departed;
and the star went before them,
till it came and stood
over where the child was.
When they saw the star,
they rejoiced with great joy.

They saw the young child
with Mary his mother,
and fell down,
and worshipped him;
and when they had opened
their treasures,
they presented unto him gifts;
gold, and frankincense,
and myrrh.

*And being warned in a dream
that they should not
return to Herod, they departed
into their own country
another way.*

*And when eight days
were accomplished,
the child's name was called
Jesus.*

*

This book was set in 14 point Janson (CRT) type by
American–Stratford Graphic Services, Inc. Color
separations were made by Princeton Polychrome Press.
It was printed on 80 lb. Moistrite Matte by Princeton
Polychrome Press and bound by A. Horowitz & Sons.
Typography by David Rogers

The drawings were done by applying watercolors
and colored pencils to Diazo prints made from the
original pencil drawings.